This book belongs to

....

LADYBIRD BOOKS
UK | USA | Canada | Ireland | Australia | India | New Zealand | South Africa

Ladybird Books is part of the Penguin Random House group of companies
whose addresses can be found at global.penguinrandomhouse.com.

www.penguin.co.uk   www.puffin.co.uk   www.ladybird.co.uk

Penguin
Random House
UK

First published 2022
001

© 2022 ABD Ltd/Ent. One UK Ltd/Hasbro
Written by Lauren Holowaty

PEPPA PIG and all related trademarks and characters TM & © 2003 Astley Baker Davies Ltd and/or Entertainment One UK Ltd.
Peppa Pig created by Mark Baker and Neville Astley. HASBRO and all related logos and trademarks TM and © 2022 Hasbro.
All rights reserved. Used with Permission.

Licensed by
Hasbro   eOne

Printed in China

The authorized representative in the EEA is Penguin Random House Ireland,
Morrison Chambers, 32 Nassau Street, Dublin D02 YH68

A CIP catalogue record for this book is available from the British Library

ISBN: 978-0-241-54332-0

All correspondence to:
Ladybird Books, Penguin Random House Children's
One Embassy Gardens, 8 Viaduct Gardens, London SW11 7BW

MIX
Paper from
responsible sources
FSC
www.fsc.org   FSC® C018179

Don't Worry, PePpa

Peppa and her family were going to Granny and Grandpa Pig's house for lunch.

"We'd better hurry," said Mummy Pig, "or we'll be late."

"Don't worry, we have plenty of time," said Daddy Pig.
"Besides, we're always early!"
"Yes, don't worry, Mummy," said Peppa. Then she
whispered, "Daddy, what does **worry** mean?"

Daddy Pig explained that a worry is something you feel unsure about. "It's when we think something not so good might happen."
"But we're always early," said Peppa. "And Granny and Grandpa won't mind even if we are late."

"No, I'm sure they won't," said Mummy Pig.
"So you don't need to worry then, Mummy?" said Peppa.
"You're right, I don't!" said Mummy Pig. "Thank you, Peppa."

As they were getting ready, Daddy Pig told Peppa that the
best thing to do when you have a worry is to tell someone.
"Share your worry with us," said Daddy Pig.
"Then . . . *poof!* Just like magic, it will disappear!"

"I shared my worry about being late," said Mummy Pig,
"and it disappeared."
"Exactly," said Daddy Pig. "Oh, look at the time! We'd better
get going or we might actually be late!"

Outside, Daddy Pig spotted a grey cloud in the sky. "Hmm," he said. "I think I might put the car roof on."

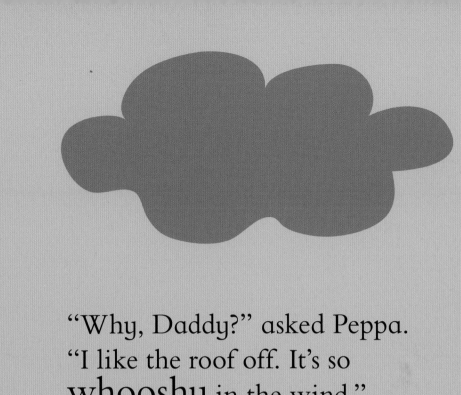

"Why, Daddy?" asked Peppa.
"I like the roof off. It's so
whooshy in the wind."
"I like it off, too, Peppa," said
Daddy Pig. "But I'm worried it
might rain, and we'll get wet."

"Don't worry, Daddy," said Peppa. "If it rains, you can
put the roof up then."
"Yes . . . I suppose I could!" said Daddy Pig.
"So you don't need to worry then, Daddy?" said Peppa.
"No, not at all," said Daddy Pig. "Thank you, Peppa."

"The best thing to do with a worry is to share it, Daddy," said Peppa. "Then . . . *poof!* Just like magic, it will disappear!"
Daddy Pig laughed. "Ho! Ho! Ho!"

"Hello, little ones," said Granny Pig
when they arrived.
"Are we late for lunch, Granny?"
asked Peppa.
"You don't need to worry – you're
always early!" said Granny Pig.
Peppa looked at Mummy Pig and smiled.
"See, Mummy?" she whispered.
Mummy Pig winked.

Peppa and George ran out into the garden.
"Hello there!" called Grandpa Pig. He was
in his shed, making a toy racing car for
Peppa and George to play with.

"*Brum! Brum!*" cheered George.

Peppa hopped in the car first and rode around the garden. She went up and down the hills, squeezing the horn. *Toot! Toot!*

Toot! Toot!

When it was George's turn to drive the car, he wasn't too sure. "What's wrong, George?" asked Grandpa Pig. "You look a bit worried."
"The best thing to do when you have a worry is to **share it**, George," said Peppa. "Then . . . *poof!* Just like magic, it will disappear!"

George pointed at a hill.
"I think George is worried
about this hill, Grandpa,"
said Peppa.

"Well, that's easy to sort," said Grandpa Pig.
"Let's take the car to a flatter part of the garden."
"*Brum! Brum!*" cheered George, zooming around
in the car. Soon, he even felt fine about the hill
and raced down it as fast as he could . . .

"I don't think George has a worry any more, Grandpa," said Peppa. "No . . . *puff* . . ." said Grandpa Pig, trying to keep up with George. "I don't think George has any worries at all!"

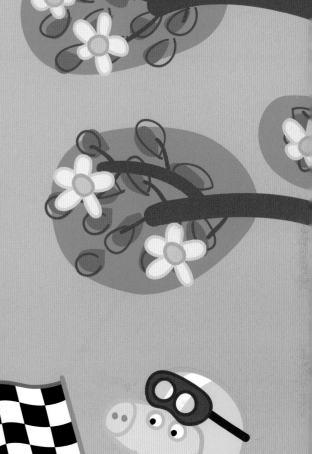
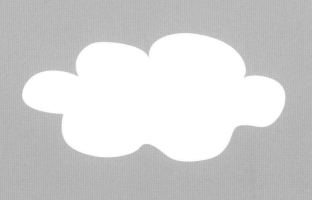

When they'd finished playing, Grandpa Pig, Peppa and George went inside for lunch.
"Yummy!" cheered Peppa. "This is delicious."
"Thank you, Peppa," said Granny Pig. "I tried a new recipe and was a bit worried how it would turn out."

"The best thing to do when you have a worry is to share it, Granny," said Peppa. "Then . . . *poof!* Just like magic, it will disappear."

"That's very true, Peppa," said Granny Pig.

As it was such a lovely afternoon,
Granny Pig suggested they eat their
cake in the garden.
"Look at that," said Mummy Pig.
"Not a cloud in the sky, Daddy Pig."
"Yes," said Daddy Pig, smiling.

"Why don't you all go outside, and I'll
bring out the cake?" said Grandpa Pig.
"Can I help, Grandpa?" asked Peppa.
"Of course, Peppa," replied Grandpa Pig.
"That's very kind!"

"Can I carry the cake, Grandpa?" asked Peppa. "It's a bit heavy," said Grandpa Pig. "But why don't you carry this very **special plate** instead?"

Grandpa Pig went outside with the cake, and Peppa followed. She felt proud to be carrying the very special plate. But just as she was about to step outside . . .

she **bumped** into a chair and dropped the plate.

SMASH!

"Oh no!" Peppa cried, looking at the broken plate.

When Peppa walked outside, her tummy felt a bit wobbly.
But then she remembered what Daddy Pig told her.
"I have a little worry, Grandpa," said Peppa.
"Well, why don't you tell me all about it so I can help you?"
said Grandpa Pig.

Peppa told Grandpa Pig about the broken plate.
"And it's your very **special** one," she said sadly.
"I'm sorry, Grandpa."

"Don't worry, Peppa," said Grandpa Pig, giving her a big cuddle. "That plate doesn't matter at all. What matters is that you're OK."

"Thank you, Grandpa," said Peppa. And . . . *poof!*

Just like magic, Peppa's little worry disappeared.

Peppa showed Grandpa Pig where the broken plate was so
he could clean it up, and then they went back outside . . .

Peppa felt much better. "Could I have a really big slice of cake, please, Granny?" she asked. "Remember, Peppa," said Daddy Pig. "The best thing to do with a cake . . . is to share it!"

"Yes, Daddy," said Peppa, giggling. "I've shared my worry, and now I'll share the cake!"
And . . . *poof!* Just like magic, Peppa's really big slice of cake disappeared!